# Turn Left, Turn Right

### by Lynn Trepicchio
### illustrated by Elene Usdin

Orlando   Boston   Dallas   Chicago   San Diego

Visit *The Learning Site!*

www.harcourtschool.com

In San Francisco there is a lot to see.
I know just how to get to my favorite
places. Come on. We'll come back to
my home in Alamo Square later.

First, we turn left at the traffic light. The cable car comes right away. It is nearly full, but we jump on and find a place to stand. My owner really likes the wind in her face.

We ride the cable car north, to the very end of the line. Everyone gets off there. I like to watch the cable car driver turn the cable car around so he can drive it back.

We turn left at the stop sign. Now we
walk east to Fisherman's Wharf. It's a
good walk for a little dog like me, but the
breeze from the bay on the left feels nice.

There's always something happening
at Fisherman's Wharf. Today it's a funny-
looking creature with hard skin. It doesn't
seem too friendly.

Lunchtime at Fisherman's Wharf is great. There are so many choices to make. Which way should we go? Turn left? Turn right? It's a difficult choice.

After a good lunch, we turn right and
look for a taxi. We ride in the taxi. It goes
west to our next stop. There we will see
the Golden Gate Bridge.

There's always something happening at this park near the bridge. Today someone is selling hot dogs. They smell so good! I wonder why they are called "hot dogs." Those silly things don't look like me at all!

This is the Golden Gate Bridge. Isn't it beautiful? Someday I want to walk across the bridge to see what's on the other side.

Some of my friends are at the park, too.
What should we do? Should we play tag
or catch? Should we just run around? It's
a difficult choice.

Snack time at the park is great. I get a
special treat, but I could really use some
water. Playing hard has made me thirsty.

So I jump up for a drink. The water is cold, but I think this is a good water bowl. It's very big. It's also very messy!

"I'm sorry," I tell my owner. She laughs
when I give her kisses. I guess she
understands. Since I'm so tired, I don't
think I can walk home. My owner knows
what to do.

First, my owner turns right at one
corner. Then, she turns left at the next one.
She crosses at the traffic light. I have
taught her well. She knows the way
home, and I can get some sleep.

# San Francisco, California

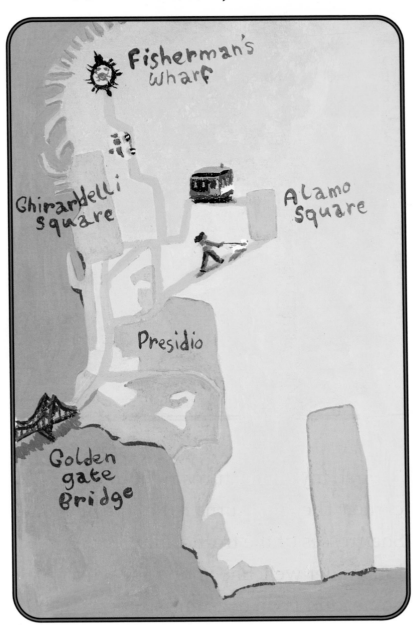